THE MESSIEST ROOM ON THE PLANET

by Monica Kulling & Nan Walker
illustrated by Jerry Smath

Kane Press, Inc.
New York

For Erica and Edwin, whose rooms were never this messy—M.K.

For the kids of Mrs. Terwelp's kindergarten class—N.W.

To my grandson Jonathan Andrew Smath—J.S.

Text copyright © 2009 by Nan Walker
Illustrations copyright © 2009 by Jerry Smath

Library of Congress Cataloging-in-Publication Data

Kulling, Monica.
    The messiest room on the planet / by Monica Kulling & Nan Walker ; illustrated by Jerry Smath.
        p. cm. — (Social studies connects)
    Summary: Anxious to enter a contest for turning a messy room into a clean one, Jon and Lucas work hard to clean Jon's very messy room but lose the contest form in the process.
    ISBN 978-1-57565-282-5 (alk. paper)
    [1. Cleanliness—Fiction. 2. Contests—Fiction.] I. Walker, Nan. II. Smath, Jerry, ill. III. Title.
    PZ7.K9490155 Mes
    [E]—dc22
                            2008026608

10 9 8 7 6 5 4 3 2 1

First published in the United States of America in 2009 by Kane Press, Inc.
Printed in Hong Kong.

Book Design: Edward Miller

Social Studies Connects is a registered trademark of Kane Press, Inc.

www.kanepress.com

"Your room is perfect, Jon." My best friend
Lucas looks around. "Just perfect!"

I stare at him. Is he kidding?

Lucas is a total neat freak. When he sees my
room, he uses words like *messy, slob,* and *gross.*

But *perfect*? That's a first.

"Okay, Lucas," I say. "What's the joke?"

He grins. "No joke. Just a chance to win a contest." He shows me a bright green piece of paper. It says, *We're searching for the messiest room on the planet!*

My room is messy. But it isn't *that* messy.

Is it?

Lucas pulls out a camera. "I'll take the Before, During, and After pictures." He snaps a photo. "There! I've got the Before shot."

"Um . . . before, during, and after *what*?" I ask.

"The cleanup!" he says. "The room that goes from messiest to cleanest wins the contest."

I gasp. *"Clean up?* When no one's making me?"

Changes take place over time. Words like **before**, **during**, and **after** help us understand changes in time.
Before: Your room is a mess.
During: You are cleaning it up.
After: It's nice and clean!

5

"Come on, Jon. I'll even help," Lucas says. "But if you win, we split the prize."

I glance at the form again. The prize is $50—and a "fabulous mystery cleaning product."

Hmm. I could use fifty bucks. Maybe Lucas will want the cleaning product. He's the neat freak, after all.

"The contest ends tomorrow," I say. "We'd better clean fast!"

Lucas nods. "I'll start with the desk. You can start under the bed."

"Do we really have to clean under the bed?" I ask. "I mean, it won't show in the picture."

He gives me a look.

Oh, fine. I look under the bed. *Ew!* Something stinks. And it's dark. "I can't see," I complain.

"Don't you have a flashlight?" says Lucas.

"Sure, somewhere." Let's see. I was using it to read in bed. Then it rolled off. . . .

I groan. "The flashlight is under the bed."

I start poking around in the dark.

Then I grab something slimy and oozy. *Ick!*
I sit up. My hand is full of rotten banana.

The camera flashes. "What a great shot! You
should see your face!" Lucas says, laughing.

If we win, he *definitely* gets the cleaning
product.

I wipe my hands on my shorts and dig under the bed again. I find a dirty sock, some little wheels, a dried-up marker— "Hey! I found the missing piece from my 3D puzzle!"

"You threw that puzzle out," Lucas reminds me. "You said it was missing a piece."

Oh. Yeah.

Lucas holds up a piece of paper. "Here's some
old math homework. There's no grade on it.
Looks like you never turned it in."

"Awesome! Maybe I can still get credit."

"I don't think so," he says. "It's from last year."

Pretty soon we have a bunch of nice neat piles—trash, recycling, stuff to give away.

Lucas snaps another shot. "Looking good."

My room really does look good. I could get used to this. Maybe I'll split the fifty bucks with Lucas after all.

Then he says, "What about the closet?"

"Wait!" I say. "I wouldn't open—"
Too late.

I look at the pile of junk. "Wow! This is just like that movie we saw where the landslide buried a whole town. Cool, huh?"

Lucas doesn't answer.

I grab his camera and snap a shot. "You should see your face!" I say.

Scowling, Lucas climbs out of the mess.

Hey! There's my gladiator costume. Wonder if it still fits.

I pull off my shorts and shirt and put on the costume. The helmet is a little tight.

"'Ake my 'icture," I say.

"What?" Lucas asks.

"'*Ake* my '*icture!*"

"*What?* I can't understand you with that helmet on."

I sigh. "All 'ight. I'll 'ake it off."

I can't! It's stuck!

As I tug at the helmet, Lucas says, "Oh! I get it. Take your *picture*!"

The camera flashes. My helmet pops off, and I fall over.

At last we're done.

"ROOM CLEANING CHAMPIONS!"
I shout in my best gladiator voice.

I pose, and Lucas takes the After shot.

We give each other a high five. Then he looks
at his watch. "Yikes! It's dinnertime. Got to run."

After Lucas goes, I flop down on my bed.

My room has never been this clean. It practically squeaks. This has got to be the cleanest room on the whole planet. I can't wait to fill out the contest entry form and send it in.

Wait a minute. Where *is* that entry form?

WE'RE SEARCHING FOR THE MESSIEST ROOM ON THE PLANET! CONTEST ENTRY FORM

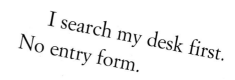

I search my desk first. No entry form.

Next I dump out the give-away bin. It's not here, either!

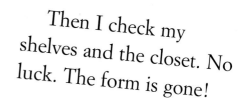

Then I check my shelves and the closet. No luck. The form is gone!

First, **next**, and **then** are more words that can help you put events in order.
For example:
First you put your right foot in.
Next you take your right foot out.
Then you do the Hokey Pokey!

19

After dinner I trudge over to see Lucas. "You don't have any more contest forms, do you?" I ask.

"Nope. I snagged the last one. Why?"

I swallow hard, then tell him I lost it.

He groans. "All these great pictures! Wasted!"

I glance at his computer screen. Wow! Was my room really that bad?

The photo shows how Jon's room looked in the **past**. The past can be just a second ago—or it can be millions of years ago! The **present** is right now. The **future** hasn't happened yet!

20

Lucas clicks to the second photo. "This one was my favorite," he says sadly.

I look, and something catches my eye.

"The form!" I point to a bright green paper on the bed. "It's not there now, though. I searched *everywhere*."

All things change over time. Jon looks at the second photo. He sees that the form was on his bed **then**. But it's not there **now**!

Lucas perks up. "Let's check the other shots."

In the third photo, the bed is made. The form is gone.

"Wait!" I say. "See what's poking out of my back pocket? Now I remember. I stuck the form there before I made the bed." I check my pocket. "There's nothing in here," I say.

One event often affects another event. Jon wanted to make his bed. So first he had to take the form off the bed and put it somewhere else.

South Regional Library
The Woodlands, TX 77380
IN TRANSIT SLIP

Transit to: FM
Transit date: 11/20/2020,
8:44
Transit library: SOUTH
Transit reason: LIBRARY
ID: 34028075827114
The messiest room on
et
er: Kullin

"Of course not," says Lucas. "You were wearing shorts. But you took them off to put on the gladiator costume. See?" He clicks to the costume picture.

"Then where did my shorts go? Here they're lying on the floor—" I click to the last shot. "And here they're gone."

"Well, sure," Lucas says. "They were covered with banana goop. I put them in the laundry."

The laundry!

> You can make a **timeline** to help put events in order!
>
> | 4th photo | 5th photo | 6th photo |
> |---|---|---|
> | Lucas opened the closet | Jon fell over | Jon posed for the After picture |

23

I race back home and run up to my room. The laundry basket isn't there.

I dash down to the basement. There's my laundry basket. Empty! And the washing machine is filling up with suds.

"NOOOOOOOOOooooooooooo!"

"Looking for something?"

My mom waves a bright green paper at me. It's the entry form!

She smiles. "I've told you a million times to check your pockets before—"

I snatch the paper, kiss her on the cheek, yell "Thank you!" and run up the stairs.

I step into my room. Yikes! What a mess I made looking for the form!

It's almost as bad as the Before photo.

I start cleaning up—again. My mom pokes her head in. "Cleaning your room without being asked? This is a first!"

Boy, you'd think I was a slob or something.

When I'm finished, it's not quite as perfect as the After photo. But it's not the messiest room on the planet, either.

Weeks go by, and I forget about the contest.
Then, one day, a big box comes with a letter
on top. I tear the letter open.
We won!

After I see what's in the box, I call Lucas.
He lets out a whoop. "I knew you'd win!"

"I couldn't have done it without you," I say.
"In fact—you can have *all* the prize money. You
earned it."

"Wow, thanks!" he says. "You should keep the
cleaning product, anyway. You need it more."

"Sounds good to me," I say. "You know . . ."

"It really is *fabulous!*"

I can order events!

So can I!

MAKING CONNECTIONS

If you think ordering events is just about history—think again! Every time you say *before* and *after,* or *first* and *last,* or *next* and *then,* you're putting events in order.

"George Washington was the president *before* John Adams." "I ate dinner. *Then* I ate dessert." See? Ordering events is a piece of cake!

Look Back
• Look at page 22. What does Jon say he did with the form *before* he made the bed?
• On page 23, where did the shorts go *after* they were on the floor?
• Read page 25. What must Jon's mom have done *before* she turned on the washing machine?

Try This!
Check out each set of pictures. Decide which picture came *before* and which one came *after.*

Set 1

Set 2

Bonus! Put these three pictures in order.